To my dogs, my friends' dogs,
and all the dogs I've ever known:
Tsetsa, Ooshik, Dasha,
Dunya, Tipsi, Milu, Pico, Mila,
Busya, Moisei, Zorro, Billo, Kyra,
Bingo, Sancho, Hemma, Schnaps,
Tobik, Winnie, Samantha,
Pete, Betta, Petunia, and Stiopa

To Evgenia, Anna, and Alexandra, and also to Masha B. (Kurochka) and Anna Alessandra S.

by Vladimir Radunsky

Harcourt Inc.

TRANSLATED FROM DOG-ESE TO ENGLISH BY MY LEARNED DOG, TSETSA

Orlando   Austin   New York   San Diego   London

Woof, woof,
bow wow,
arf, arf,
bow wow!

Here I am, alone in the park.
No owner. No leash. No collar.

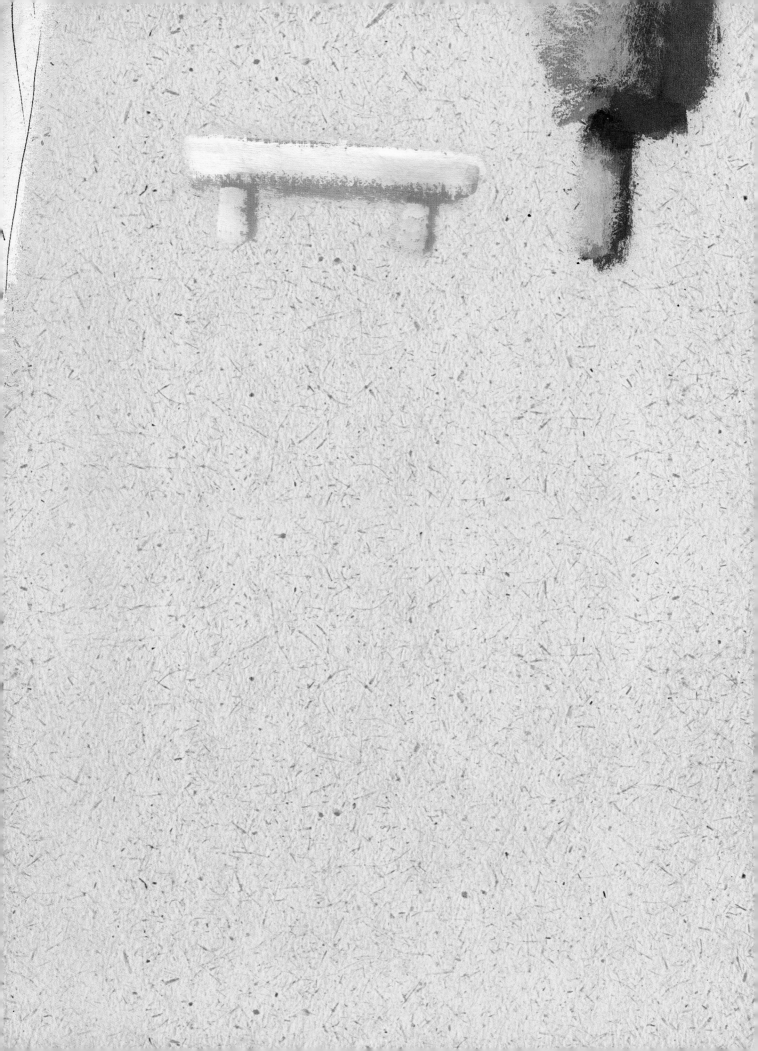

Here I am, alone in the park.
No dog. No friends. No fun.

You look solid!
Too bad you already have a dog.
A big, strong dog!
No, you wouldn't want me.
I'm not that strong.

Yip,yip,yip,yip,
yip,yip,yip, arf!

Ooh! You're wonderful!
What cute chubby cheeks!
Too bad you already have an owner.
I want you!

And what about you, Mr. Whitepants?
You already have a dog, too?
It looks like everybody has a dog these days.

Woof, woof, bow wow?
Arf, arf, yip, yip, yip?
Bow wow.

I want you! White.
With a little black spot.
I'd like to take you home.
White. With a little black spot.

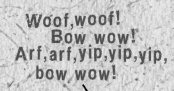

Woof, woof!
Bow wow!
Arf, arf, yip, yip, yip,
bow wow!

I love you, Ms. Bluehead-Yellowsquares-Redstockings!
If you take me with you, I'll dye my ears blue!

I like you and your bird.
The cats could have your dog, and I could have you!
I'd even build a nest on your head.

Bow wow!
Woof, woof. Arf..

You like cats? I like cats, too.
I want you and your cats, all three of you!

Poor old doggie, you have beautiful eyes. I want you.
I would never leave you, even for a minute.

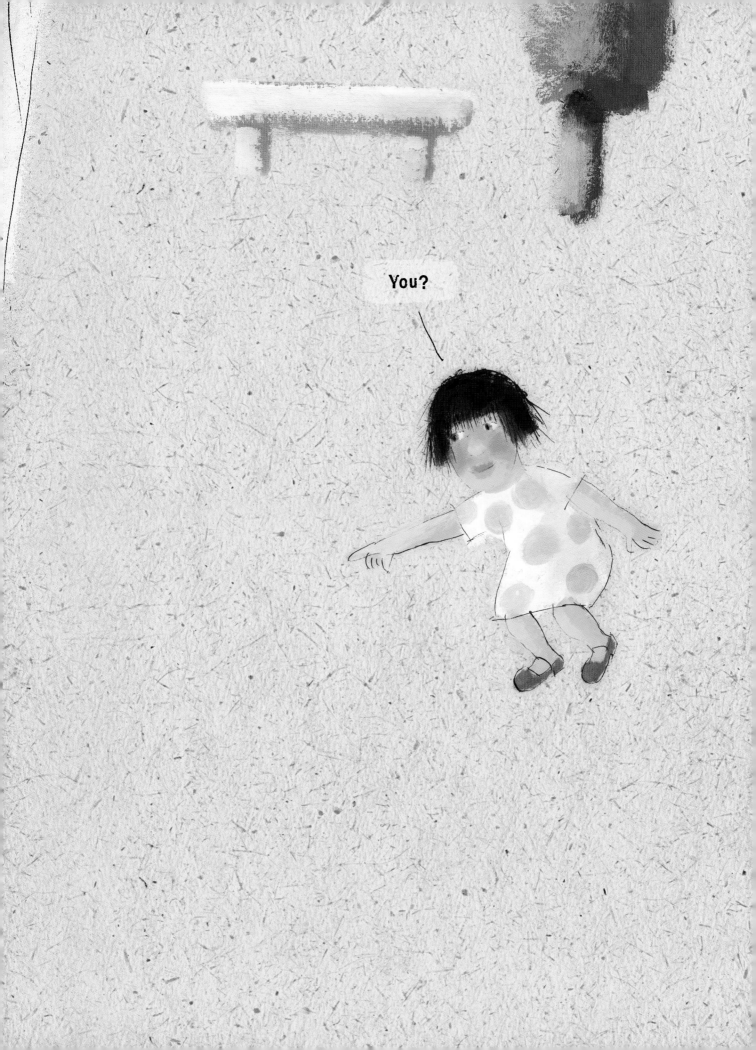

YOU!

Library of Congress Cataloging-in-Publication Data: Radunsky, Vladimir. You?/V. Radunsky. p. cm.

Summary: A lonely girl and a stray dog find one another in a park. [1. Dogs—Fiction. 2. Human-animal relationships—Fiction.] I. Title.

PZ7.R1226You 2009 [E]—dc22 2008003281 ISBN 978-0-15-205177-8

First edition H G F E D C B A

Printed in Singapore

The illustrations in this book were done in gouache on handmade paper.

The type was set in Ratbag.

Prepress by Studio Punto Rome.

Color separations by Colourscan Co. Pte. Ltd., Singapore

Printed and bound by Tien Wah Press, Singapore

Production supervision by Pascha Gerlinger

Designed by Vladimir Radunsky